FOREVER STAR

Gareth Peter **and** Judi Abbot

PUFFIN

For my very own Forever Stars . . .
Anthony and Noah – G.P.

To Massimo, the King of France,
with love – J.A.

PUFFIN BOOKS

UK | USA | Canada | Ireland | Australia | India | New Zealand | South Africa

Puffin Books is part of the Penguin Random House group of companies
whose addresses can be found at global.penguinrandomhouse.com.

www.penguin.co.uk   www.puffin.co.uk   www.ladybird.co.uk

First published 2021
001

Text copyright © Gareth Peter, 2021
Illustrations copyright © Judi Abbot, 2021

The moral right of the author and illustrator has been asserted

Printed in China

The authorized representative in the EEA is Penguin Random House Ireland,
Morrison Chambers, 32 Nassau Street, Dublin, D02 YH68

A CIP catalogue record for this book is available from the British Library

ISBN: 978–0–241–45302–5

All correspondence to: Puffin Books, Penguin Random House Children's
One Embassy Gardens, 8 Viaduct Gardens, London SW11 7BW

This is the dark and starless sky,
where just past the moon a planet drifts by.

And this is the planet that's full to the brim
with friendly and caring space people called . . .

... TIM!

These are the Tims,
busy working away ...

But here is one Tim who's not happy today.

He longs to have children, but that makes him sad,
as most homes, he thinks, have a mum and a dad . . .

This is Tim's husband, who squeezes his hand,
and says, "We would be the best dads in the land!
Children want safety – they need to feel *love*,
in a home that fits snugly, like wearing a glove.

It just doesn't matter how parents are paired
as long as that love is eternally shared."

So they hop on their space bikes

and off they both *fly* . . .

. . . to speak with the Space Queen, beyond the night sky.

"Magnificent Space Queen – please grant us our dream.
We wish to be parents, we make a great team.
Please can we adopt? There's room in our heart
to *welcome* a child who needs a new start."

This is the Space Queen,
who thinks for a while.

"A child
with *two*
dads . . ."

"Yes,"
she says with a smile.

"Just give them a home that is full to the brim
with cuddles and kindness . . .
and two dads called Tim!

So now, with my blessing, go into the night
and search for your star child – the one that's just right."

They pass comets and rainbows,

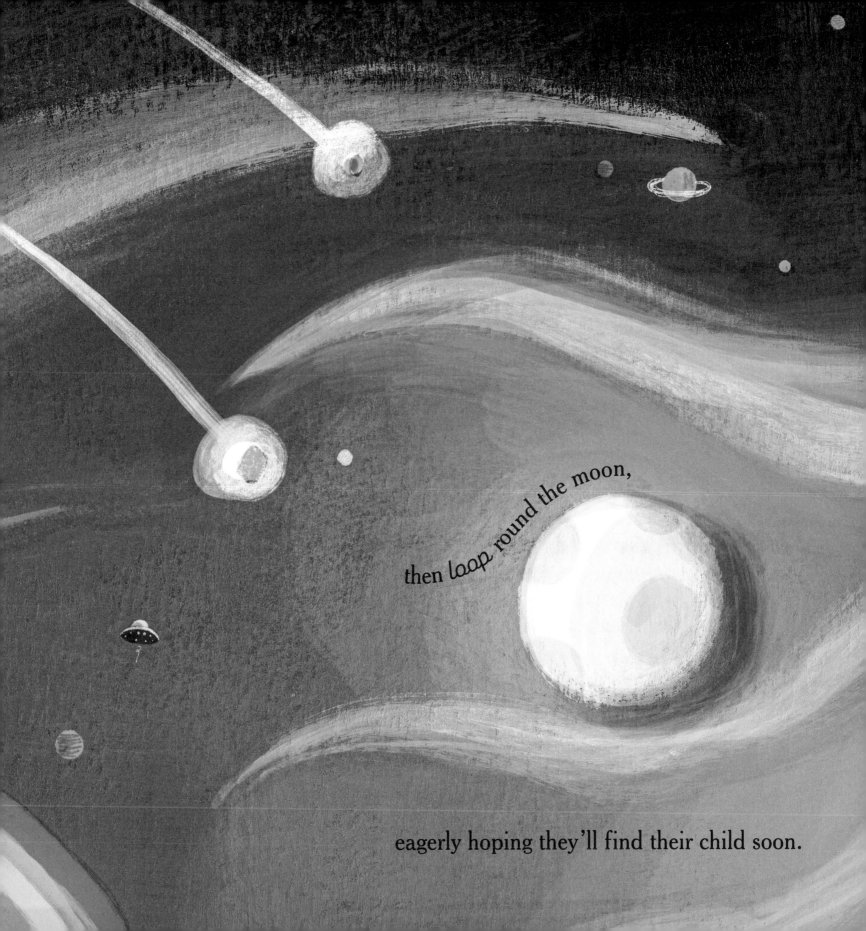

then *loop* round the moon,

eagerly hoping they'll find their child soon.

As meteors tumble, they whirl and weave by,

past
great
supernovas
that
speckle
the
sky.

They almost lose hope,
but then deep in the night . . .
they spot a small planet
that's beaming with light.

This is the planet, where children can play,
who don't have a forever place they can stay.

And this is Miss Foster, who cares for them all,

whether quiet

or noisy

or teeny

or tall.

She says, "There is someone here, just right for you,
who longs for a home that is right for them too."
The Tims join the picnic, then realize: that light
is the glow of a child . . . Could this one be right?

Tim's tummy tingles. "I think that's our boy!
Our very own starlight, our very own joy."

Delighted, Miss Foster says,
"That's Little Jim.
He's friendly and caring – let's go and meet him."

This is the boy who is nervous inside . . .

But who runs to the Tims
with a smile he can't hide.

Tim says, "There's a room just for you and your toys.
We'll make lots of cakes, you can make lots of noise."

Every night we can read. Every day we can play.
And this home's *forever* . . . Shall we go there today?"

This is the boy who then thinks for a while . . .
"A home with *two* dads . . ."

"Yes," he says with a smile.
"A forever family! I've dreamed of this day.
I love to read stories . . . I can't wait to play."

So they set off together, as Jim waves goodbye,
to start a new life underneath a new sky.

These are the dads flying home with their son,
excited and scared that this journey's begun . . .

Looking forward to
birthdays and trips
to the sea,

exploring new moons,
planting their family tree,

planning sun days
and fun days,

quiet days

and loud . . .

Sharing sad times and glad times, and times to be proud.

"We travelled through space, beyond Neptune and Mars.
And we'd do it again – for a family like ours."

This is the son with two dads by his bed.

"Sweet dreams, little star child, and lay down your head.
Our life was complete the first time we met you.
Now wherever you are – your dads will be too."

This is the dark and *star-filled* sky,
where just past the moon a planet drifts by.

And this is the planet that's full to the brim . . .

With two loving dads and *me* . . .
Little Jim.

So, when you gaze up at the dark evening sky,
at every bright twinkle or spark flashing by . . .
That's the light of a parent, who's travelled so far,
to find their own wonderful *forever star.*